Ted and Ned Adopt a Kitten

T, D, N Sounds

By Cass Kim, M.A. CCC-SLP
Illustrated by Kawena VK

Ted and Tina Adopt a Kitten

T, D, N Sounds

P.A.C.B. Speech Sounds Series

This is a work of fiction. Names, characters, places, and incidents either are the
product of the author's imagination or are used fictitiously. Any resemblance to actual
persons, livir   r dead, events, or locales is entirely coincidental.

Cover Design by: Kawena VK

Illustrations by: Kawena VK

Non-Commercial Use Copyright: Kawena VK

Illustration Commercial Use Copyright: Cass Kim

For Leland and Harper and the many adventures you will have together.

Hello I'm Ted!
And this is my sister, Tina.
We both put our tongue tips behind our front
teeth to say our names.

It just takes a quick tap – you try! Three taps.
One - Ta!
Two - Ta!
Three - Ta!
Nice work.

Guess what? Today, Dad is taking us to get a pet!
We thought for two entire nights about what type to get.
It's a very big decision, you know.

Dad had many ideas, mostly for pets
that live in tanks.
Like hamsters,
fish,
and even a turtle!

Tina said, "No thank you."
She did not want a turtle.
Would you want a turtle?

I thought I wanted a dog.
But then Dad said we would have to walk it,
Brush it,
and feed it twice a day.

That's a lot of work.

So I decided not to get a dog.

Tina and I thought and thought and thought...

Until... finally... we knew.

We want a kitten.

We want a cute, tiny, nice, playful kitten.

So today Dad is taking us to the shelter to
pick out our new kitten.
Or maybe we will get a grown-up cat.
He said we can play with lots of cats and
kittens until we find the perfect one.

Inside the cat room at the shelter
there are so many cats and kittens.

Big cats,

small cats,

kittens,

and old cats.

Playful cats,

sleepy cats,

snuggly cats,

and pouncy cats.

The cats have so many different types of fur.
I never knew before that they could all look
and be so different.
It is wonderful.

Can you show me the brown cat?

Now the orange cat.

How about the small black cat?

Do you see the white and tan kitten?

Look very carefully.

He is hiding.

The white and tan kitten is under the table.

"Kitten" and "table" both use tongue taps. Just like Tina and Ted!

I tap the tip of my tongue behind my teeth for the end of "kitten" and at the start of "table."

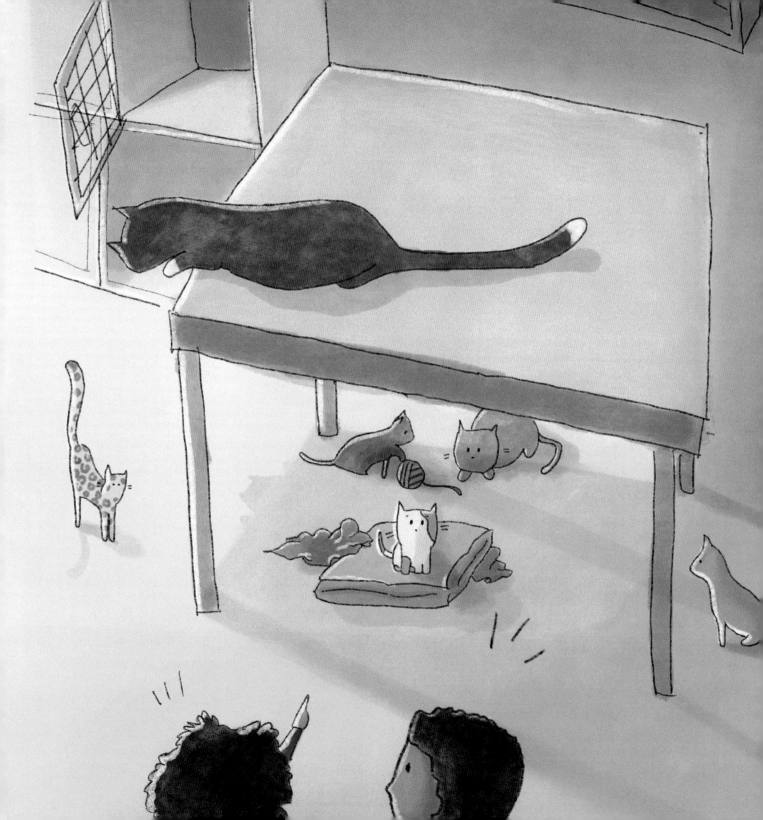

Tina and I both want to hold the white and tan kitten.
Dad helps us get him out from under the table.

He is soft.

He is cuddly.

He is perfect for us.

Now we need to decide on a name for him.

What do you think is a good name?

Tina and I want his name to tap our tongues, just like our names.

Let's name him Ned!

Ned the Kitten.

Time to go home. Thanks for coming with us to the shelter.

Can't wait to talk again soon!

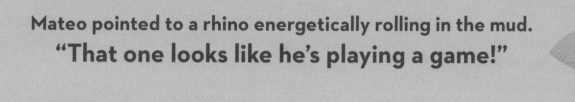

Mateo pointed to a rhino energetically rolling in the mud.
"That one looks like he's playing a game!"

"Good eye!" said David.
"That rhino's name is Jeremiah, and he is
missing his left front foot. It was most likely
caught in a poacher's snare trap.

"Many of the animals here are not quite
the way God originally created them to be,
whether from injuries or illnesses."

Mrs. Chen chimed in,
"Does anyone remember what big event
happened after creation?"

Willow, who was usually quiet, spoke up. "The fall."

Mrs. Chen said, "Why yes, Willow, the fall! When Adam and Eve disobeyed God,
the whole world was changed. Everything that had once been purely good
now had something else too: sin, disease, and death."

David continued, "As you can see, Jeremiah doesn't let
his injury stop him from enjoying life. He's having a blast
while accomplishing the same task as the other rhinos."

Willow turned her head, revealing a
large brown birthmark on the side of her face.

"Of course Jeremiah still enjoys life!
A lot of people think having a difference
with your body means you can't be happy.
But that's wrong!

Life is beautiful,
even when it has hard things in it.

And like Mrs. Chen said before,
all people are worthy of honor and respect,
regardless of the ways they may be different."

Everyone was silent for a moment,
taking in Willow's unexpected speech.

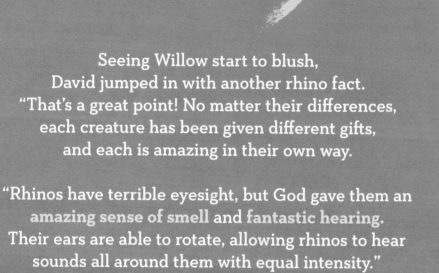

Seeing Willow start to blush,
David jumped in with another rhino fact.
"That's a great point! No matter their differences,
each creature has been given different gifts,
and each is amazing in their own way.

"Rhinos have terrible eyesight, but God gave them an
amazing sense of smell and fantastic hearing.
Their ears are able to rotate, allowing rhinos to hear
sounds all around them with equal intensity."

Mateo whispered to Ruthie,
"I've never heard Willow talk so much before!
I always thought her birthmark was
kind of cool, like Zoe's white fur."

"Oh sure," Ruthie snapped.
"Willow's birthmark is cool because it's different,
but I just have ordinary old freckles."

sniff

"Here's number three of the Big Five!"
David exclaimed.

A herd of elephants grew larger by the minute as the Jeeps drove closer.

Bobby said, "Look at that smaller elephant—
its ears are so big for its head!"

Several of the other boys laughed, and Mateo's ears reddened,
as if they'd been teasing him instead of the elephant.

David said, "That elephant does have big ears!
His name is Charlie, and I bet he loves his big ears.

Elephants' ears help protect them from the sun's heat,
just like a beach umbrella.

"And the ears of an elephant are also used
for communication, so Charlie is one of the
chief leaders for this group."

Wow, thought Mateo, Charlie uses his big ears to do a lot of important things.
But what are my big ears good for?
After thinking for a few minutes, Mateo tapped Ruthie on the shoulder.
Ruthie didn't respond, but Mateo spoke anyway.

"I'm sorry for not listening to you very well.
How my ears look was more important to me than using them
for what God created them to do. If I'd been really listening to you,
I wouldn't have tried to make the conversation all about me."

Ruthie turned around. "I forgive you, Mateo." Smiling a bit, she added,
"And it's about time you put those ears to good use!"

Her smile faded
as she thought,
*But there couldn't
possibly be any good use
for frizzy hair and freckles . . .*
She stared at her appearance in the
side view mirror of the Jeep.

"Quick, look to the right!"
David pointed to a lioness
darting through the tall grass.

Bobby exclaimed,
"Wow! She's so fast.
That's cool to see her charging at full speed!"

David nodded. "Sophia, our speedy lioness,
is number four on the Big Five list! We've almost seen them all now."

Just then, Ruthie stopped staring at herself in the side view mirror.
"Huh? Number four? Where? What was it?"

Mateo looked at her with wide eyes.
"You missed the lioness?! She was unbelievable."

Mrs. Chen gently added, "Mirrors can be funny things. Often the
more time you spend looking into them, the less you really see."

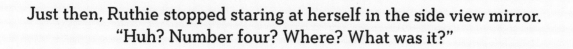

Ruthie looked down.
"You're right. I've been thinking
so much about how I look, I've hardly
enjoyed this trip and now I've missed
seeing something amazing!"

Turning to Mateo, she added,
"I owe you an apology too.
I'm sorry for being mean to you to
get back at you for hurting my feelings."

"Number five of the Big Five, the African buffalo!"
David announced.

"If you look ahead, you'll see a small herd
of them. It appears they have formed a circle
around a few other buffalo."

Bobby raised his hand.
"Why did they do that?"

David smiled and continued,
"They do this to protect the buffalo
that are young, old, or injured.
The stronger ones point their horns
toward the predators. This keeps
predators from reaching the animals
that aren't strong enough to fight."

Mateo said to Ruthie,
**"Wow! I wish people were more like buffalo. Instead of
sticking together, we usually pick on people who are weaker."**

"I know someone who is like the buffalo," said Mrs. Chen.
"Or rather, the buffalo are like him."

"Him who?" asked Bobby, ever curious.

Mrs. Chen quickly responded,
"God of course! Remember, all creation reflects
something of his character, since he is its Maker.

"In the Psalms he is described as
'a father to the fatherless, a defender of widows.'
And in Jesus we see even more clearly God's care
for people who are weak or suffering."

Just as Mrs. Chen finished, they pulled up to the Welcome Center.
"Class, let's thank David for a great trip!"

"Thank you, David!"
shouted all of the kids as they jumped off the Jeep and ran toward their bus.

As they left the safari park, the bus hummed with
excitement. All the children recounted the sights from that
day, trying to decide which animal was their favorite.

Mrs. Chen raised her hand to
gather the students' attention.

"Would anyone like
to share something
they learned today
about God's creation?"

"It's amazing!"
shouted Bobby.

"That's certainly true," agreed Mrs. Chen.
"But can you be more specific? What was so amazing about it?"

"Well, even though all of the creatures God made have different shapes, sizes, and abilities, they each have exactly what they need. And their differences make the world a really interesting place to live!" Bobby explained.

Mateo added, "But we also saw a lot of animals who are suffering because of the fall. Even though God made the world good, everything isn't good all the time anymore."

Ruthie raised her hand. "I liked what Willow said, though, about animals and people being able to still have a beautiful life, even when things aren't quite right. And that God has given each of us special gifts!" After a pause, she added, "I also learned that it's important to pay attention to the beauty all around us, because it can be easy to miss!"

"Yeah," Mateo agreed. "We get to use our bodies for the purposes God created them for so we can enjoy and take care of each other and the rest of the world too!"

Willow spoke up once more.
**"Because of what Jesus has done as our Savior,
God makes us more and more like him—glorious images of God."**

Giraffe

The name giraffe is derived from the Arab word *zarafa*, which means "the one who walks very fast."

Giraffes don't drink much water. This is because they get most of their water from their leafy meals and only need to drink once every few days.

Leopard

African leopards have strong legs that help them run at speeds of up to 36 miles per hour. They can leap vertically up to 10 feet in the air to catch a bird and horizontally up to 20 feet to cross obstacles.

The eyes of the African leopard are capable of seeing seven times better than human vision in the dark.

Rhinoceros

Rhinos are known for their giant horns that grow from their snouts, hence the name rhinoceros meaning "nose horn." African black rhinos have two horns.

Elephant

Elephants have an amazing memory. Upon the return of a long-lost friend, elephants perform a joyous greeting ceremony where they spin in circles, flap their ears, and trumpet.

Elephants' trunks are strong enough to pull down trees and delicate enough to pick up a tiny twig. When crossing deep rivers, elephants even use their trunks as built-in snorkels!

Lion

A male lion's roar can be heard from up to five miles away, the loudest roar of any big cat species. But unlike house cats, lions can't purr.

A lion can see five to six times better than humans, but when they are born, they are blind.

African buffalo

The African buffalo is the only species of wild cattle that can be found in Africa. They have horns shaped like question marks.

African buffalo have poor eyesight and hearing, but their sense of smell is excellent.

Africa's Little Five

See if you can find these famous African wild animals hiding as Mrs. Chen's class drives by!

Elephant Shrew

Ant Lion

Rhinoceros Beetle

Buffalo Weaver

Leopard Tortoise

Dear Parent or Caregiver,

Thank you for reading *God Made Me in His Image* to your child. We wrote this book as a tool so you can explain to your children that God made their bodies and this is foundational for their self-image. In a generation overflowing with negative body-image messages, children's body image is an urgent issue. Children need to know God made their bodies and made them special. The message children need to hear is this: "God made you in his image. Every part of your body is good because God made every part and called them all good."

Our goal is that the message of this book will encourage them to appreciate their bodies and address the questions and shame regarding them. This is important because research regarding children and body issues is staggering and sad. Children are dealing with body-image distortion at an early age. Many young children are dieting or developing dangerous eating habits. Additionally, many trends in our culture lead to hypersexualizing of children.

- Five-year-old girls whose mothers reported current or recent dieting were more than twice as likely to have ideas about dieting than girls whose mothers did not diet. A mother's dieting behavior is a source of her daughter's ideas, concepts, and beliefs surrounding dieting and body image.[1]

- By age six, girls especially start to express concerns about their weight or shape.[2] Almost half of American children between first and third grade are worried about how much they weigh,[3] and half of nine- to ten-year-old girls are dieting.[4] Approximately 80 percent of all ten-year-old girls have dieted at least once in their lives.[5] Even among underweight to average-sized girls, over one-third report dieting.[6]

- By the age of ten, around one-third of all girls and 22 percent of boys say how their bodies look is their number one worry.[7] Age ten is also the average age when children start dieting.[8] Girls have always shown greater concern about their weight and appearance, but there is a significant increase recently in boys also worrying. Boys want to be tall and muscular—and they worry about weight too.

- Childhood obesity has tripled since the eighties.[9]

- Virtually every media form studied provides ample evidence of the sexualization of women and men, including television, music videos, music lyrics, movies, magazines, sports media, video games, the internet, and advertising. Children internalize this message.

Research shows that elementary school age is when children are at risk of developing a poor body image. By helping to improve their body image at this stage and making them more aware of messages the media is putting out, parents and caregivers can equip them better to be confident about their bodies.

Parents are one of the most powerful influences in children's lives regarding their body image. This book serves as a tool to start the conversation about the practical body-image implications of being made in God's image.

Thank you for taking the time to read this book and talk to your child about it.

Best,
Lindsey and Justin Holcomb

Encouraging Children to Have a Healthy Body Image

- Encourage children not to compare themselves to their peers. Instead, help them give thanks to God for the gifts he has given to them, and ask God to show them how they can become more like him today.

- If your child has a physical impairment, remind him or her it does not negate your child's inherent worth as God's image bearer, nor does it diminish the other qualities God has blessed your child with.

- Help victims of bullying boost confidence by focusing on how much they're worth because they are made in the image of God and by reminding them of the positive attributes God has given to them. Also discuss strategies for how they can respond to bullying the next time it occurs, and seek out additional resources on bullying to help you support your children.

- Encourage your children to do the things they love that are good. Spending time on worthwhile activities boosts confidence and builds healthy friendships.

- With your children, make a list of new things they want to try, learn, or tackle. Learning how to use their bodies in new ways can give them a greater appreciation for its capabilities and remind them that God gave them their bodies to be used to do good things.

- Set a positive example by not criticizing other people's bodies. If children see their parents judging appearances, then they will be much more likely to do the same to others and themselves.

- If you have insecurities about your appearance, don't make offhand, critical comments about those perceived flaws around your children. Instead, intentionally talk with your children about how God has helped you learn to see your body more like the way he sees it, even though you still forget to see your body that way sometimes.

God's Good Promises for You

God will love you forever.
Give thanks to the Lord, because he is good. His faithful love continues forever. Psalm 136:1

God will comfort you.
The Lord will comfort his people. He will show his tender love to those who are suffering. Isaiah 49:13

God will keep you safe.
When people are in trouble, they can go to him for safety. Nahum 1:7

1. Things I can do well, right now . . .

2. Things I can't do yet, but am working on . . .

3. New things I want to try or learn . . .

4. What do I need to do to start learning and trying those things?

1 Beth A. Abramovitz and Leann L. Burch, "Five-year Old Girls' Ideas About Dieting are Predicted by Their Mothers' Dieting," *Journal of the American Dietetic Association* 100, no. 10 (October 2000): 1157–1163.

2 "What Are Eating Disorders?," National Eating Disorders Association, accessed March 23, 2020, http://www.nationaleatingdisorders.org/get-facts-eating-disorders.

3 Ibid.

4 M. E. Collins, "Body figure perceptions and preferences among pre-adolescent children," *International Journal of Eating Disorders*, 10(2), (1991): 199-208.

5 L. Mellin, S. McNutt, Y. Hu, G. B. Schreiber, P. Crawford, E. Obarzanek, "A longitudinal study of the dietary practices of black and white girls 9 and 10 years old at enrollment: The NHLBI growth and health study," *Journal of Adolescent Health* 20, no. 1(1997): 27–37.

6 J. Kevin Thompson and Linda Smolak, eds., *Body image, eating disorders, and obesity in youth: Assessment, prevention, and treatment* (Washington, DC: American Psychological Association, 2009), 47–76.

7 Nicky Hutchinson and Chris Calland, *Body Image in the Primary School: A Self-Esteem Approach to Building Body Confidence* (England, UK: Routledge, 2019), 5–6.

8 Ibid.

9 Jennifer Bishop, Rebecca Middendorf, Tori Babin, Wilma Tilson, *Childhood Obesity*, Assistant Secretary for Planning and Evaluation, US Department of Health and Human Services, updated May 1, 2005, http://aspe.hhs.gov/health/reports/child_obesity/.

New Growth Press, Greensboro, NC 27404
Text Copyright © 2021 by Lindsey A. Holcomb and Justin S. Holcomb
Illustration Copyright © 2021 by Trish Mahoney

Unless otherwise noted, all Scripture quotations were taken from The Holy Bible, New International Version® NIV® Copyright © 1973, 1978, 1984, 2011 by Biblica, Inc.™ Scripture marked with * are taken from the NEW INTERNATIONAL READER'S VERSION® NIrV® Copyright © 1995, 1996, 1998, 2014 by Biblica, Inc.®. Used by permission. All rights reserved worldwide.

Art and Design: Trish Mahoney

ISBN: 978-1-64507-076-4

Library of Congress Cataloging-in-Publication Data on file
Names: Holcomb, Justin S., 1973- author. | Holcomb, Lindsey A., 1981-
    author. | Mahoney, Trish, illustrator.
Title: God made me in his image : helping children appreciate their bodies
    / Justin S. Holcomb, Lindsey A. Holcomb, Trish Mahoney.
Description: Greensboro : New Growth Press, 2021. | Series: God made me |
    Audience: Ages 4-8 | Summary: "This simply-told story helps parents
    teach kids that God not only created their bodies, but he made them in
    his image"-- Provided by publisher.
Identifiers: LCCN 2020045152 | ISBN 9781645070764 (hardback)
Subjects: LCSH: Creation--Study and teaching. | Human body--Religious
    aspects--Christianity--Study and teaching.
Classification: LCC BS651 .H65 2021 | DDC 233/.11--dc23
LC record available at https://lccn.loc.gov/2020045152

Printed in Canada

28 27 26 25 24 23 22 21   1 2 3 4 5